SOMEWHERE

ROBIE H. HARRIS

art by ARMANDO MARIÑO

CANDLEWICK PRESS

Somewhere.
Somewhere is
where I wanted to go.
Somewhere new.
Somewhere
I had never, ever been before.

So I gave my daddy a big hug
and said, "Goodbye."
"See you soon," said Daddy.
I knew he would miss me,
but I had to go.

And off I went,
step-by-step,
making footprints
in the mud.

I didn't know where I was going.
But I knew I was going somewhere.

So I kept on going.

Along the way, I found a shiny peso!
And a big green leaf!
So I picked them up
and walked some more.

Then I found a pretty white flower!
And three fluffy feathers!
I picked them up, too,
and kept on walking.

Suddenly, I was somewhere.
Somewhere new.
Somewhere so nice.
Somewhere so quiet.

I was very sure Daddy
would love it here.
With me.

"Daddy!" I called.
"I'm somewhere!"

Daddy didn't answer.
Maybe he didn't hear me.
I was sure he was lonely
without me.

So I had to go back to Daddy.

"Go . . ." I muttered. "Just go . . ."
But I couldn't.
So I hollered, "GO NOW GO!"
And off I went.

First I went one way.
Then another way.
I was all mixed up!
I didn't know which way to go.

Then I saw some footprints.
Muddy footprints.
My footprints!
And I knew just what to do.

Follow my footprints!
Step-by-step.

And there was my daddy
waiting for me!
I ran so fast
and jumped into his arms.

Daddy gave me the biggest hug.
"Welcome back," he said.
"I missed you!
I knew you'd come back.
But where did you go?"

"I just went somewhere," I said.
"Somewhere new.
Somewhere I've never been before.

"I brought you a shiny peso,
a big green leaf,
a pretty white flower,
and three fluffy feathers."

"I love everything you brought me," said Daddy.
"But most of all—I love you!"

"Daddy," I said.
"Let's go somewhere."
"OK," he said. "Let's go!"

So I took my daddy's hand,
and off we went.

Somewhere.
Somewhere we had never,
ever been before.

For Sam, Ella, Daisy, and Rosie—
for inspiring my stories
RHH

To my sons, Alessandro
and Valentino
AM

First edition 2022

Library of Congress Catalog Card Number pending
ISBN 978-1-5362-0735-4

21 22 23 24 25 26 APS 10 9 8 7 6 5 4 3 2 1

Printed in Humen, Dongguan, China

This book was typeset in Rialto.
The illustrations were done in watercolor and ink.

Candlewick Press
99 Dover Street
Somerville, Massachusetts 02144

www.candlewick.com